SECRET FC

SECRET FC

TOM PALMER

With illustrations by
Garry Parsons

Conkers

First published in 2013 in Great Britain by
Barrington Stoke Ltd
18 Walker Street, Edinburgh, EH3 7LP

www.barringtonstoke.co.uk

This edition first published in 2017
Reprinted 2019, 2021

This story was originally published in a different form as
The Secret Football Club (Puffin, 2010)

Text © 2013 Tom Palmer
Illustrations © 2013 Garry Parsons

A CIP catalogue record for this book is available
from the British Library upon request

ISBN: 978-1-78112-687-5

Printed and bound by CPI Group (UK) Ltd, Croydon, CR0 4YY

For Iris, the best daughter in the world

CONTENTS

Chapter 1

The Railway Children

It was the first day back at school after the summer break. Six weeks of fun and holidays over. Finished.

But Lily, Zack and Khal weren't sad to be back. They were over the moon.

The three of them stood in the playground and looked round the school grounds. Nothing had changed. Kingsfolly Junior School was just as it had always been.

The school building was old and brown. The small car park was packed with teachers' cars. The woods over beyond the playground were as dark and creepy as ever. And the playground itself was marked out as a football pitch, ready for the first game of term.

"Kick off at morning break?" Lily asked.

Zack and Khal nodded.

Zack was short and stocky, with dark hair in tight plaits. Khal was tall and had a thin face.

"Yeah," Khal said. "I can't wait."

"Nor me," Zack agreed.

Lily pushed her curly blonde hair away from her face. "It's been a long time since we played football," she said.

And it had been a long time. A *very* long time.

Kingsfolly Junior School was in the middle of the city. The triangle of ground on which it sat had a very busy road on one side, and several railway tracks on the other two. Trains thundered past the school every couple of minutes.

The part of the city Lily and the others lived in was so built-up that there was no room for fields and parks. No room for football. There were just houses and shops and warehouses and roads and railways, all packed in together.

There was only one place children could play football without being flattened by trains and cars. The school playground.

And that was why they were all so excited about being back at school. They hadn't played a proper game of football for weeks!

Every time they'd passed Kingsfolly in the holidays they'd gazed at the playground and wished they could go in and play. But there was no way they could get over the 4-metre fence that protected it from the outside world.

Zack rubbed his hands together and grinned. "Did you see that Jag in the car park?" he asked.

"No," Khal said. "No kidding? A Jag?"

Another voice spoke over the racket of shouting and screaming in the playground. "*I* saw it. It's an F-type."

A girl with long dark hair in dreadlocks came and stood next to Lily. She was Lily's best friend, Maddie.

"Do you reckon it's his?" Lily said.

"Whose?" Zack asked.

"His!" said Lily. "The new Head Teacher. Mr Whatshisname."

"Edwards," said Maddie. "Mr Edwards. Has anyone seen him?"

Everyone shook their heads.

"Well he must be cool if he's got an F-type," Khal said, just as the school bell went off.

"We'll find out in assembly," said Lily. "It starts in five minutes."

And the four friends headed into the school, full of hopes for the new Head Teacher and the new term.

Chapter 2
Double Trouble

"Good morning, children," the new Head Teacher said.

"Good-mor-ning-Mis-ter-Ed-wards," 120 voices chanted back.

Mr Edwards nodded and gazed around the school hall. His eyes travelled over the cheerful murals on the walls and the wooden floor. Everything was gleaming, ready for the new term.

The new Head was a short, bald man. He had on a thick black suit and glasses. As Lily watched him, she noticed that he had not yet smiled. She remembered the last Head Teacher – Mrs Warner. She had *always* smiled.

Lily elbowed Zack. "Ask him." She grinned.

"What?" Zack said.

"If it's his car. The F-type."

Zack shook his head and looked down as Mr Edwards' eyes flicked towards him. Then the new Head stared at all the students.

"Before we sing," he said, "I have a few things to say."

Lily looked around at the rest of the students and teachers. There was something *strange* about the mood in the hall today. Something different to

how it had been last term. But what was it? And why?

"First of all, thank you for your welcome this morning," Mr Edwards said. "I am very happy to be your new Head Teacher."

Lily thought he didn't sound happy at all. His voice was hard and cold.

"Second, I want to let you know that the school marks its 100th birthday in October. And I have asked Mrs Baker to think up a way to mark this as she has been here the longest of all of the teachers. I'd like you all to support her as much as you can."

Lily looked at Mrs Baker, who was their class teacher this year. Mrs Baker was nice. Everyone liked her. But even she wasn't smiling today. Not

even when Mr Edwards had mentioned her and everyone was looking at her.

Lily felt panic rise in her chest. Something was wrong. She could sense it.

Mr Edwards' voice was even harder than before when he spoke again. "Last of all," he said, "I need to remind students that there was a series of injuries in the playground last year. Some parents have expressed concerns and this has resulted in a change in school rules. From now on, football – and all other ball games – are banned from the school grounds."

There was a huge gasp, then silence for two or three seconds. It was as if everyone was holding their breath. This news was so sudden. So unexpected.

Mr Edwards paused. "I am sorry about this," he said. "But I have a duty of care to you and I must protect you from dangerous activities and the serious injuries you could suffer playing football."

Lily felt her head go hot inside. And then she realised that she was on her feet. The only child out of all the school.

Mr Edwards looked at her over his glasses. "Yes?"

"You can't," Lily said in a whisper.

"I can," the Head Teacher said. "And I will."

Then Lily felt a hand on her arm. It was Mrs Baker.

"Sit down, Lily," Mrs Baker said in a kind, but very firm voice.

Lily sat. She could feel her eyes beginning to sting. There was a thick lump in her throat. Her face itched.

Mr Edwards looked at Lily for a second more. There was an uncomfortable silence. Then he nodded to Mr Nokes at the piano.

"Now for our first song," he said as music filled the hall and everyone stood to sing.

Chapter 3

Dead Ball

At break, Lily, Maddie, Zack and Khal gathered at the far edge of the playground where the woods stretched to the back of the school grounds.

They were joined by James and Batts.

They had planned to meet here to play football. But that wasn't going to happen. Not now.

Lily eyed James as he came over. He had light brown hair and was the tallest boy in Year 6. Lily liked him, even though he always seemed to want

to argue with her. She hoped they could be on the same side in this business.

No football! No football for the rest of the year. No football *ever*! Lily couldn't imagine living in a world like that.

"What are we gonna do?" Batts asked as he and James joined the circle of friends. He was big for a Year 6 too, with hair that was always shaved ultra-short. "This is stupid ... It's ..." Batts fell silent, at a loss for words.

Lily looked blank.

"She's still upset," Maddie explained to Batts and James.

"I'm upset too. We're all upset," said James. He looked cross. "You're not the only one who gets to be upset, Lily."

Lily shrugged again. "I didn't say I was."

James crossed his arms. Lily wondered why he was always so angry.

Then Zack spoke. He'd been gazing into the woods up to this point. But now he was looking at his friends.

"We need to stop feeling angry and sad," he said. "We need to think of a way of getting football back instead."

Lily nodded. "Zack's right. We need a plan."

James stepped forward. "Yeah!"

"But what plan?" Khal asked. "Mr Edwards looks like he's never changed his mind about anything."

"Well, he's going to change his mind about this," Maddie said. "Isn't he, Lily?"

Lily nodded. "He is. But how?"

"Did Mrs Baker talk to you in assembly?" Zack asked.

"Yes," Lily said. "But only to tell me to sit down."

No one spoke for a few seconds. They were all thinking hard. Most of them were staring into the woods, as if the answer was in there. But it didn't seem to be. And even if it was, they wouldn't be allowed in to find it! They were banned from the woods too. That was a ban that had been in place long before Mr Edwards had come along to spoil their lives.

The woods *were* part of the school grounds. And children *used* to be allowed in them. Zack's dad had been a pupil at the school when he was young and said he remembered playing there. Climbing trees. Making dens. That sort of thing.

But now the woods were out of bounds until the school could raise the money to clear the ground to make them safe. No one ever went in there. Well, almost no one.

Lily was still thinking when she noticed that Zack was staring at her.

"What?" she asked.

"Maybe she's the answer," he said.

"Who?" Lily asked. What had they been talking about? Their teacher? And then she twigged. "Mrs Baker! That's it! She'll help us! She'll tell Mr Deadwards where to go! She's not afraid of anyone."

Once the others had stopped laughing at Lily's nickname for the new Head Teacher, they all began to nod.

"That's it," said Khal.

"Do it," said Batts.

James just shrugged.

"Who's coming with me, then?" Lily asked.

Lily didn't really need to ask. She knew that she had all of them with her as she walked across the playground towards the classroom.

Chapter 4

Reading the Game

"I'm sorry, children. I've talked to Mr Edwards about it and I won't ask him again." Mrs Baker looked them in the eye one by one as she broke the bad news. She had a soft voice, dark hair and eyes that normally sparkled. Today, she just looked tired.

They had asked as soon as Mrs Baker came back to the classroom after morning break.

"But, Mrs Baker ..." Lily said, then stopped. She realised she was about to cry. And she didn't want to cry in front of the class.

She felt so sad. She loved football. They all did. When would they ever get to play it again if they weren't allowed to play at school?

Never. That was when!

Lily went to her seat and shrugged when she saw the others looking at her from their tables. Zack sat next to her without a word.

"Now, Year 6, today we're going to be talking about ... history!" Mrs Baker announced.

Lily heard Khal and Maddie groan. Then she glanced across at Oliver Sykes. He had sat up and was looking eager, like a dog about to get a biscuit. 'Typical Oliver,' she thought. Oliver was always

interested, no matter what lesson they were doing. Except in P.E. He was one of those boys who loved school work and hated games – especially football. Lily didn't understand at all.

"We're going to be looking at the history ..." Mrs Baker went on, "of football!"

Lily looked up. Had she heard Mrs Baker right?

"What?" Khal asked. He looked confused.

"The history of football, Khalid," Mrs Baker repeated.

Then everyone was listening to the most unexpected history lesson they'd ever had.

"Football used to be played *not* on pitches – *nor* in playgrounds – but across fields and ditches and hedges," Mrs Baker told them. "More than 500 years ago it was played village against village. Games

would last all day in some cases. And lots of people from each village would play. Sometimes hundreds. They played with special, decorated balls."

Lily was listening with a frown on her face. What was this all about? She looked over at Oliver. He looked back at her, frowning too. Then Lily saw a grin creep across Khal's face.

Maybe this was going to be a *good* history lesson.

Their teacher went on to explain that the game in the olden days was called mob football or folk football. But sometimes it got so violent that people had broken legs and arms – and had even died – playing it.

"And in 1314 it was banned," Mrs Baker finished.

The room was quiet for a few seconds. Mrs Baker was looking at the children as if she wanted them to say something. But no one did. So she went on.

"King Edward II banned it because he thought it was too dangerous. There were other reasons, but that was the main thing."

"It's like Mr Edwards here," James muttered.

Mrs Baker paused.

"What were the other reasons?" Zack asked. His eyes caught Lily's.

"Well, one reason was he wanted his people to practise archery, not football. They used bows and arrows in all the wars that they used to fight then."

"So did they stop playing?" Batts asked.

"Good question," Mrs Baker replied. "What do *you* think?"

"I suppose if the King said they couldn't play, then they didn't play," Oliver Sykes said.

Mrs Baker shook her head. "No," she said. "Even with the threat of prison, they carried on playing."

Mrs Baker paused again. Again, no one filled the silence. And Lily caught James looking at her, puzzled.

"Now, can you remember what Mr Edwards said in assembly?" Mrs Baker asked.

No one spoke. Then Oliver smiled. "That football in the playground is banned," he said.

"Thank you, Oliver," Mrs Baker said. "But not *that*. What did he say about the school's 100th birthday?"

"That we need to celebrate it," Maddie said.

Lily looked down at her exercise book. The subject had gone off football. And she was sad again.

"And that I am to plan the activities we do?" Mrs Baker reminded them.

No one answered her.

"Well, I think that each class should celebrate by dressing in the clothes of a different century. What do you think?"

"Great," Oliver said.

"And *you*," the teacher went on, "could dress up as people from the ... 14th century."

Lily stared at the table. Why was Mrs Baker so bothered about dressing up in silly costumes? And what had the 14th century got to do with anything? It was *football* that was important.

Chapter 5

Journey to the Centre of the Earth

"What was Mrs Baker on about?" Maddie asked when they were gathered – as always – at the far edge of the wood.

Lily shrugged and looked at Zack and Khal.

"I'm not sure," Zack said. "But I think she was making a point of some kind."

They stared into the woods.

James and Batts came over, so that now all six of them were standing together.

The noise from the playground was as loud as usual. Younger kids ran around and chased each other. Older ones stood in groups. There was not a ball in sight.

"Let's go into the woods," Khal said.

"Do we dare?" Lily asked. She looked round for one of the teachers on duty.

"I don't think we should," Maddie said.

"I dare," said James.

"So do I," said Lily.

"No you don't."

"I do."

"Prove it."

They'd been into the woods before. After the summer holidays last year, they had sneaked in there and built a den. Just the six of them.

"Mr Edwards won't like it, will he?" Maddie said, looking at Lily.

"So what? He's not the King, is he?" James said. "And he never said we couldn't go into the woods. Maybe that rule has been forgotten."

"Come on then," Batts said.

Without another word the six children ran along the side of the old sheds and slipped one by one into the woods. They walked through the trees and hanging ivy and over what looked like an old tennis court that was now overgrown. The court was crumbling as tree roots burst through its surface.

They found their den. It was a shack they'd built with huge old pieces of corrugated iron and sheets of plastic they'd found in the woods. Everything was just as they'd left it. No one had been inside.

Nothing had been moved. They went in and sat in a circle.

Lily was first to break the silence. "What are we going to do?" she asked. "About football?"

"Nothing," James said. "We can't do anything."

"We have to," said Khal.

"But what?" Maddie moaned. "There's nowhere we can play. Not round where any of us live. And now not in school. We'll never be able to play football again in our lives."

"But what if Mrs Baker was trying to tell us something with all that history stuff?" Zack said.

Lily looked at Zack. If anyone was going to solve their problem it was him. Zack was clever. He always found ways to solve problems.

"But what?" she asked again.

"Well … if it was OK to carry on playing football in the 14th century," Zack said, "then maybe it's OK now too. Maybe Mr Edwards is just a stupid king."

"Mrs Baker didn't say that," James cut in.

"But maybe that's what she meant," Lily said. She could see what Zack was getting at now.

"So how are we going to play football?" James demanded, with a scowl at Lily. "It's not like you can put up a massive screen in front of Mr Edwards' office so he can't see us play in the playground. And there's nowhere else to play. Not for miles."

No one answered. James was right.

Lily looked at her watch. She felt sad again. "We have to go back before the end of lunch," she said.

The six of them stood and ducked out of the den. Lily waited until James was well ahead before she followed on. He was really getting to her.

They all walked carefully back across the old tennis court, trying not to get their legs caught in the tangle of ivy and tree roots.

They were almost out of the wood when Lily realised someone was missing.

"Where's Zack?" she asked.

They were all worried. Maybe he'd fallen and got injured. And they'd left him there!

Lily led them back. When they reached the clearing where the old tennis court used to be, they saw him.

He was standing in the middle of the court with great clumps of ivy and roots in his hands.

Lily and Maddie looked at each other. James put his hands on his hips.

"Have you gone mad, Zack?" he asked.

Zack beamed at them.

"This is it," he said. "This is where we can play football. Hidden by a screen. Of trees!"

Chapter 6

Dirty Beasts

For the next two weeks the six children worked every hour they could.

Every break.

Every dinner-time.

Because Zack had had a brilliant idea. The old tennis court was perfect for a football pitch. A *secret* football pitch.

The surface of the court had been broken up by roots and was covered with ivy and other plants, but

it was still a flat surface and it was as big as a five-a-side pitch.

And the best thing? It was hidden from the school by the dozens of trees in Kingsfolly Wood.

Zack had worked out a system.

Each break and dinner-time, four of them would go into the woods and clear the court. The other two would act as lookouts. One guarded their way into the woods. The other watched the school buildings – including Mr Edwards' office window which had a view over the woods.

That was how they would protect the Secret Football Club.

Clearing the court was hard. Hard *work*, and also hard to stay clean when they were busy moving plants and soil around.

In the first couple of days they had smuggled in garden tools from their parents' houses. There were small saws to hack out roots and shears to cut small branches and tough stems. And then there were trowels, the only digging implements small enough to get into their school bags.

They cut and dug and slashed and chopped and hacked. But by the Friday of the first week the tennis court looked no different, except that there were huge piles of dead plants and wood at the side.

"This'll take all year," Maddie moaned.

"Maybe all term?" Lily smiled back at her friend. "But it'll be worth it. Imagine having our own secret football pitch."

And so they kept at it.

It was hard not to get dirty, but Zack came up with a system for that too.

First, everyone brought in spare clothes to put over their school uniforms as they worked.

Second, the person guarding the way into the woods had to inspect the four clearing the woods on their way out to check if they were too dirty. If they were, they would have to wash at the handy outdoor tap at the back of the old sheds.

They knew only too well that if they were seen to be dirty – or with torn clothes – the teachers would suspect something was going on.

The work went on for two weeks.

Around the middle of the second week, there was a dramatic change. All of a sudden the tennis

court was clear. They could see how big it was. Now they were levelling off the pitch instead of clearing weeds and roots. They focused on finding soil and small stones deeper in the woods to fill holes in the court's surface.

One day it rained and that was a big help, letting them press mud into the cracks the ivy had torn up.

On the second Friday of term, Khal was starting to get fed up.

"Let's play at afternoon break today," he said. "It's ready."

"Not yet," said James. "It's not perfect."

For once Lily agreed with James. "We need to level off the bottom end first," she said. "James is right."

Khal started to climb one of the trees by the pitch. "It's level," he said. "I can see it from here. From above." He climbed higher.

"It's not level," Zack said. "One more day and it'll be right."

They all gazed down the pitch. It was good. But *not* perfect.

As they gazed away from Khal and the tree he was climbing, they heard the noise. A sharp crack that echoed around the wood.

And, when they looked round, they saw Khal on the ground with his eyes closed and a large branch on top of him.

Chapter 7

Don't Tell the Teacher

Once Khal's eyes had opened, James took over.

First, he talked to Khal to make sure he was OK. Then he checked all Khal's limbs, to make sure there were no breaks or deep cuts. The other four held their breath.

The only thing James could find wrong was a rip in Khal's trousers and a nasty cut on his shin.

"You need to get that cleaned up and dressed," James said.

"It'll be OK," Khal said. He winced as he straightened his leg.

"James is right," Lily said. "It could go bad."

James nodded.

"How do you know about all this, James?" Maddie asked.

"Scouts," he said. "We did a First Aid course."

They helped Khal across the playground. All the other children in school stopped to stare. They formed a pathway between the woods and the main door.

All the way, Lily's tummy was churning. She could see teachers' faces at some of the windows on the second floor. And Oliver Sykes was watching them, on his own at the edge of the playground.

They'd need to reveal their secret to make sure Khal got looked after properly, Lily thought. How

else could they explain his fall – and how dirty he was? Then there'd be no football ever again. Full stop.

Mrs Baker was the first to the door.

"What's happened?" she asked.

Lily said what they'd agreed to say. "We were behind the sheds – and Khal fell."

"Let's take a look," said Mrs Baker. "Bring him up to the sick bay. Can he walk?"

"With some help," Lily said.

With Maddie on one side and James on the other, Khal limped up the stairs.

This was going OK so far, Lily thought. Mrs Baker wasn't asking any more questions. And no other teachers had got involved.

They made it up the short stairs to the sick bay. Maddie, James and Lily crowded round the doorway. Zack and Batts stood on tip-toes behind them.

Mrs Baker looked at Khal's leg, then at the others.

"You lot go back to the playground," she said. "I'll look after Khal. It's not serious."

But then they heard another voice. A man's voice. It was Mr Edwards.

"What is going on?" he demanded. "How did this happen? Why are you all so filthy? What have you children been doing?"

Mr Edwards looked suddenly worried. "Khalid? Are you OK?"

"He's fine, Mr Edwards," Mrs Baker said. She smiled up at the Head Teacher.

Mr Edwards looked relieved. Then he said, "Lily? Were you there?" He bent down so his face was just centimetres from hers.

Lily tried to step backwards. "Yes," she answered.

This was it, she thought. This was where she was going to get told off and found out and everything else. It was the end. How else could they explain the soil on their hands? They hadn't had a chance to wash since Khal fell out of the tree.

Mrs Baker broke in. "It's OK, Mr Edwards," she said, her voice calm. "Khal has grazed his knee. It's only a small cut. Lily and the others helped him up and into school. And they've all got a bit dirty in the process."

Mr Edwards didn't look very convinced. He frowned at Lily. Lily was almost sure he knew about the tennis court. About the Secret Football Club. About *everything*.

"I'm more concerned about Khal's knee than a bit of dirt," Mrs Baker went on. "Mr Edwards, can you please get me some bandages from the supply cupboard?"

With that, Mr Edwards became Mrs Baker's nursing assistant.

And the Secret Football Club was *still* secret. And ready for their first game of the season next Monday!

Chapter 8

Offside

Khal eased himself back into a soft chair as his classmates went back to their Maths lesson. He could have gone to Maths and coped with the pain from his sore shin, but this was nicer. Much nicer. He had a glass of milk, a banana and a chocolate biscuit left over from lunch. And his phone in his pocket. Why go to Maths?

In the small office next door, Mrs Baker was talking to Mr Edwards. Mr Edwards was pacing up and down in front of the desk. He looked worried.

"Tell me again how it happened," he said.

"Khal fell. He just tripped over. It happens every dinner-time. To someone."

Mr Edwards stopped pacing and stood still. "I know," he said.

Mrs Baker paused for a moment to look out of the window. Then she spoke again. "You do get terribly worried when the children are in danger, don't you?"

Mr Edwards sighed. "Yes," he admitted.

"What is it?"

"What's what?"

"Why do you get so worried? Children play games and fall over all the time. It's part of growing up."

"It's ... Well ..." Mr Edwards stuttered. "You're thinking about the way I banned football on my first day, aren't you?"

Mrs Baker nodded.

"I knew you were against me on that," Mr Edwards said, "but it's for their own good."

"It's not that I'm against you, Mr Edwards. I will support any of your decisions. I just don't understand why you made *that* decision."

"I should explain."

"That would help," Mrs Baker agreed.

"When I was about ten," Mr Edwards said, "the same age as Lily and Khalid and their friends ..."

"Yes?"

"... I played football all day. I loved football. I was good at it."

Mrs Baker looked confused. "Then why ...?"

"Why did I ban football?"

"Yes."

Mr Edwards breathed in. Mrs Baker could see that he was struggling to explain himself.

"Because," he said at last, "that summer – when I was ten – I was playing football with my best friend, Peter. In some fields near where we lived. And ..." Mr Edwards swallowed. "Peter tripped on a heap of dumped bricks hidden in some long grass. And he fell. He hurt his head and his neck. And ... he was paralysed. For the rest of his life."

Mrs Baker nodded, but she didn't speak. She couldn't – she was working too hard to stop the tears forming in her eyes.

Chapter 9

Friendly Matches

On Monday morning Lily arrived at the playground early.

She was too excited not to be at school. She couldn't wait for first break. When she came in the high gate she expected to be the first there.

But she wasn't.

James was there. Talking to Batts.

Maddie was there. With Khal. And Zack.

When they all turned to grin at her, she grinned back. This was it! There was just one more thing to decide.

"Who else do we let play?" Lily asked.

"No one," James said right away.

"Three-a-side isn't enough," said Maddie.

James shook his head. "But we'll never be able to trust anyone to keep our secret."

Lily realised that everyone was looking at her. "We need two more," she said. But then she paused. She didn't want to fall out with James before the first match. "You pick them, James."

James looked rather pleased and even more chuffed when everyone agreed. He thought for a minute. Then he said "Finn and Becky."

Now they only had to wait until 10.30 before the Secret Football Club could play the first game!

They picked two teams without wasting any time. Lily, Maddie, Zack and Finn versus James, Batts, Khal and Becky.

Then Lily said, "I declare the Secret Football Club open!" and they kicked off.

Everything was perfect.

The ball bounced well off their new surface. The only hard thing was not to make any noise. They'd decided to play in silence to protect their secret.

Playing in the woods was brilliant. All round them were trees heavy with leaves, turning a nice orange colour. The smell of earth and the plants

they'd cut filled the air. They could even hear the sound of birds over the thunder of express trains.

At first James' team was on top. With Batts in defence (and as goalie when needed) and Khal up front, they were the perfect four-a-side team. Khal scored first after a great pass from Becky.

But then everything changed – Lily and Maddie made sure of that. Once they got going, they were hard to stop.

Lily passed to Maddie. Maddie passed to Lily. Goal one!

Then, once they had the ball back, it was Lily to Maddie ... to Zack ... to Finn ... to Maddie and it was 2–1!

Lily could see James getting mad now that his team was losing. Normally he would shout at his

team and order them about. But he couldn't do that in the woods. So he had to go up to them and tell them – in a normal voice – what to do.

And that left holes in their defence. Which allowed Maddie to score again.

3–1!

"This isn't fair," James shouted.

"Shhhhhhh," said Lily.

"No way," James hissed. "You can't have Lily and Maddie on the same team. They're too good."

Zack watched as Lily, then Khal, tried to calm James down. He knew James hated losing. He always got upset if things were going against him.

Zack looked up at the outline of the school behind the trees, as a train whooshed past on the railway tracks. He hoped another train had been

coming by when James had shouted. The last thing they wanted was to draw attention to their game. They had to be hidden and quiet to get away with it.

And you could never be sure if someone was listening – or not.

Chapter 10

The Secret Football Club

That week at the end of September was one of the best Lily and her friends could remember. They weren't just playing football – they were playing *secret football*.

And secret football was special. It felt good to know that only eight of them were in on the secret. So was playing under the nose of Mr Edwards!

But they didn't neglect school. They worked hard in class and then they worked hard on the pitch. Morning break. Dinner-time. Afternoon break.

The score after the first week was 32–30 to James' team. Really close – and really exciting.

Mrs Baker was still teaching them about the 14th century. And that was what they decided to do for the school's 100th anniversary.

Mrs Baker helped the children design the costumes and Maddie's mum cut out the patterns for rough trousers and tops that might have been worn in the 14th century. Then the children had to sew their own trousers and shirts together.

Zack said they should dress up as mob footballers and re-enact a game. And – to everyone's

surprise – Mrs Baker agreed. She said it was history, and so it was fine.

Lily looked over at Oliver Sykes as Mrs Baker agreed. She could see him frowning. She even felt a bit sorry for him, he hated sport so much.

The game that lunch-time was very one-sided. Lily was determined to get back into the lead. She spent all morning firing up her team, so they could hit James' team hard.

And they did.

15 minutes into the lunch-break game they were level at 32–32. 15 minutes after that it was 36–32 to Lily's side. And Lily had scored every goal.

When she scored their 36th goal she noticed that James had gone red in the face. She knew

that was a bad sign. If James was red in the face something dangerous might be about to happen.

And it did.

James started to shout at his team.

"Batts! What are you doing? You're supposed to be a defender. And Khal, you haven't scored all day. You're supposed to be a striker. So strike!"

Lily ran over to James.

"Stop shouting, will you? They'll hear you."

"I won't!" James said, still shouting. "It's all very well for you to say 'stop shouting', but you're not getting hammered. You're winning!"

Once James had finished, Zack put his hand up. He was looking back at the playground.

"I can see two dinner ladies looking in," he said. "Hit the ground."

Everyone fell down onto the pitch, even James. They knew that they could have been heard shouting. And if they had, the Secret Football Club would be in grave danger.

They lay there for five minutes, waiting to see if anyone would come to look for them.

But nobody did. So they all stood up and walked carefully off the pitch, out of the woods, across the playground and into school.

Chapter 11

Foul Play

"Before we sing," Mr Edwards said, "I have a few announcements."

It was Friday morning assembly.

"First," he said, "plans are going well for the school's 100th anniversary on 10th October. Mrs Baker is organising a wonderful series of fancy dress projects with all the classes. I'm sure it's going to be a day to remember."

Lily smiled at Zack. She couldn't wait to dress up as a 14th century footballer!

"Second," Mr Edwards said, "the chess team had a great win last night. They reached the final of the city chess challenge. Well done, team!"

Applause crackled round the school hall. Lily grimaced. She wished she could be soaking up applause for how well her team was doing against James and his lot. But Mr Edwards knew nothing about that.

"And finally ..." Mr Edwards said. His smile slipped. "The dinner ladies have made me aware that voices were heard in the woods yesterday." He paused, then went on. "I am investigating, but I need to remind you *please* not to go in the woods. They are out of bounds. They are dangerous. And if you

see or hear anyone else in the woods, please tell a teacher or dinner lady right away."

Lily could feel the colour draining from her face. She decided not to look at James, even though she was furious with him. It was his shouting that had led to this.

Her mind was darting everywhere. What did Mr Edwards mean when he said he was investigating?

She wanted morning break to come. And soon.

They stood in silence when they gathered at break-time.

No one wanted to blame James, even though it was his fault.

Lily wanted James to say sorry. Then they would be able to move on. But she knew he wouldn't. And

she knew no one else would push him. It was down to her to get them through this.

"I think ..." Lily began. "I think that we should all take the blame for Mr Edwards hearing us in the woods."

She saw James look at her as if he thought this was a trick and she was going to turn on him any minute.

"We all need to make sure we don't get angry," Lily said. "*And* that we don't make each other angry." She looked at the others. Maddie was smiling at her. So was Zack.

Lily saw that now everyone was watching her and James. It was as if they were somehow leaders and it was up to them if they played or not.

Then she saw a smile on James' face. So she smiled back at him.

"I agree," Batts said.

"Me too," Maddie said.

Lily and James both nodded. The rest of Secret FC cheered.

They would play. They couldn't not. They loved it too much. And the problems they had were forgotten.

Once they were on the pitch, Lily felt great, even though James' team had hit back with three goals and the score was now only 36–35. She was happy because she was doing what she loved. With her friends. And her friends included James.

A short pass from Zack came to Lily's feet. She trapped it and looked up. James and Batts were in front of her. Maddie was ahead of them.

For a second she watched the trees waving in the breeze and a light shower of leaves fall on their pitch. Then she chipped the ball over the heads of James and Batts to Maddie.

Maddie turned with the ball and slotted it past Batts.

Goal!

Things were good again.

For now.

Chapter 12

Gathering Storm

Mr Edwards stared out of his office window, thinking. He'd been at the school for five weeks now and he felt he was on top of things. He had shown that he was in charge. That was important.

He glanced at his Jaguar in the car park. It was safe, he knew. But he always had to check.

He liked the school. He was happy. Even though there were cars and trains and buildings everywhere, the woods meant there were lots of

birds as well. Sometimes he watched them through his binoculars. He liked birds. He liked to drive out into the country at the weekend to spot rare waders and geese. He remembered how he had started watching birds after he no longer had his friend, Peter, to play football with as a child. After the accident.

Mr Edwards' mind flitted from birds to his pupils. They were nice kids and he liked them too. A part of him regretted the start he'd made with them. Banning football. It was not a good way to endear himself to 120 children. But it had to be done. For safety reasons. So there could be no accidents.

As he gazed into the trees, he saw a movement – a flash of colour among the trees. Was it the red

throat of a swallow? Surely it was too late in the year for swallows? The leaves were coming off the trees now. It was autumn. The swallows would have all flown back to South Africa for the winter.

He got out his binoculars.

It wasn't a swallow. There were people in the woods!

He dashed to the door. Who were these people? They could be a threat to the children, and anyone who was a threat to the safety of the children had to be stopped. He hated to see children in danger. It was why he had become a Head Teacher – to look after children.

Mr Edwards ran to the staff room, calling to other teachers. As he reached the school doors and

ran out across the playground, four teachers and a caretaker ran along behind him.

Everything in the playground looked OK. But he was worried something was happening among the trees.

Mr Edwards ran round the back of the sheds. He worked his way through the undergrowth, careful of the dead leaves under his feet. The other teachers were just behind him.

He stopped.

At first he felt relieved. It was just eight of his children, playing football. A part of him wanted to laugh and let them carry on. But he knew he had to show that he was in charge.

That was his job, after all.

At first Lily didn't realise that Mr Edwards had discovered the Secret Football Club. She played a perfect pass to Maddie, but instead of going on to score, Maddie stopped and let the ball roll away.

When Lily saw that Maddie was staring in horror at something behind Lily, she turned. And then she saw the teachers and dinner ladies standing panting on the edge of the tennis court.

Nobody spoke for a few seconds.

And in that little moment of time, Lily realised it was all over. The football. The club. The secret pitch.

And who knew what would happen to them for breaking so many school rules.

Chapter 13

Striking Out

Back in his office, Mr Edwards stood with the eight children who he had caught playing football.

What should he do with them? He had to be firm. He had told them that playing football at school was banned. If he didn't enforce the ban, he would lose everyone's respect.

And a small part of him wished he hadn't banned football at all.

"You have all broken two school rules," he said in a low voice. "One – you are not allowed in the woods. Two – you are not allowed to play football on school property."

Mr Edwards looked out of the window at the trees. He wondered how long this had been going on. It was the first time he'd seen them, but he felt sure this was not the first time they had played.

And as he stared at the trees, he saw a red and orange shower of leaves fall in a gust of wind. That was why he'd seen them. It was autumn. The trees were losing their leaves. The leaves had hidden them until now.

Mr Edwards almost smiled at the cleverness of their plan. But now he had to be the Head Teacher. He had to appear firm.

"I will be phoning all your parents and asking them to come in so I can speak to them," he said. "This is a very serious matter."

He looked at the children. Their faces were pale. At least two of them looked like they were going to cry.

After the children had gone, Mr Edwards sat at his desk and sighed. This whole business was upsetting him deeply. It had brought back bad memories – memories he'd tried to forget.

He closed his eyes and saw two clear images of his friend the day he was injured. In one image Peter was lying still after he had fallen and the young Mr Edwards had thought he was dead. In the other, Peter was running alongside him down the

wing, then playing the ball to his feet, for him to score.

It was only when Mrs Baker cleared her throat that he saw her at the door. How long had she been standing there?

"I knocked," she said.

"I'm sorry," said Mr Edwards. "I was miles away."

"I wanted to speak to you," she said, "about Lily and her friends."

Mr Edwards nodded. "I know."

And he gazed out of the window again.

This was supposed to be a happy time as the school marked its 100th anniversary, he thought. Not a sad time with crying children. He wished his friend Peter was here. Maybe he would have a good

idea how Mr Edwards could find a way of solving this problem.

Chapter 14

Unbearable

Lily felt stupid as she put on her 14th century clothes for the school celebration. She didn't feel like celebrating anything – certainly nothing to do with school.

Any day now her mum and dad were going to get a call from Mr Edwards. All weekend she'd been trying to work out how to tell them.

So what if the TV news were coming to film them? Mr Edwards had said he wanted everyone

on their best behaviour, to show Kingsfolly Junior School to be the best school in the town. Lily wasn't sure it *was* the best school. How could it be if they weren't allowed to play football?

All the year groups were mixed up at the school gates and the whole school looked ridiculous. There were First World War soldiers talking to astronauts and Victorian beggars arguing with Vikings.

It just made Lily even madder. This whole anniversary was a joke. A farce.

Mrs Baker spoke to the class before the event began.

"You all look wonderful," she said. "The perfect 14th century football team."

Maddie looked up from picking at her dress.

"That is what you are, isn't it?" Mrs Baker asked.

"We might as well be," Lily said, "seeing as we've been banned just like the 14th century players." She saw Zack and Khal nod in agreement.

"Well, I think you look great. But you need one more thing," Mrs Baker said. And she lifted a football out of her bag. But it wasn't a normal football. It was painted. Blue and yellow and white. With beautiful writing saying 'Kingsfolly FC'.

The class stared.

"Remember I told you about the 14th century footballers?" Mrs Baker said.

"The ones who were banned?" Khal asked.

"Yes. The ones who were banned. But who carried on playing."

Lily smiled as Mrs Baker caught her eye.

"Didn't I say that they played with decorated balls?"

"Yes," said Maddie.

"Well, this is *your* ball. Just for the photographs, you understand. And the TV cameras."

As the rest of the class nodded, fireworks went off in Lily's head. She'd had an idea.

In the playground each year group was asked to stand in their place.

The TV people had arrived. And so had lots of parents who had been invited to watch the celebrations. The TV footage was going to go out live on a morning news show.

Each year group was asked to stage a short re-enactment of their time in history.

The parents watched.

The cameras filmed.

Mr Edwards smiled. This was making the school look good. Like a nice school, just as he wanted.

When it came to Year 6's turn, Lily was meant to start the play. The idea was that they should throw the ball around, to show how mob footballers dressed, and what their ball looked like.

The TV man put his thumbs up to tell them to start.

But Lily didn't feel right. She'd never been on TV before. The idea of millions of people watching her made her feel very nervous. And she knew she had something she needed to do.

So she sat down. On the ball.

"And what is it *you're* doing?" the TV interviewer asked. She looked slightly uneasy.

"We're 14th century mob footballers," Lily said. "But King Edward has banned us from playing football. So we can't re-enact the game any more."

"But you can pretend today, can't you?" The TV interviewer smiled. "It's not like football is banned at this school, is it? In the 21st century?"

For a second, Lily didn't know what to say.

Chapter 15

Let's Play

The TV camera team turned to Mr Edwards, who was standing behind them.

"You're the head of this school, aren't you?" the interviewer asked. "Mr Edwards, right?"

Mr Edwards nodded.

"And is football really banned here?"

"It is," he replied.

The interviewer turned to Lily. "And how do you feel about that?"

"Sad," said Lily.

"I'll bet," said the interviewer. "Mr Edwards, may we ask *why* football is banned at your school?"

"Because it's dangerous. And I do not want my children hurt."

"But surely it's only football?"

"People can still get hurt," Mr Edwards said.

"But people can get hurt crossing roads or opening doors," the interviewer said. "Surely football's no more dangerous than anything else?"

"We have no playing fields at this school," Mr Edwards said. "If we did, then it would be possible. But all we have is this small playground. And it is up to me to protect everyone in the playground. A playground that is shared by Years 1 to 6, I

should add. And I choose to offer that protection by banning ball games."

No one spoke for a few seconds.

Then another voice cut in. It was Oliver Sykes. "You could play in the woods," he said. "For the re-enactment."

Lily stared at Oliver. Oliver the football hater – suggesting they should be allowed to play football? Oliver smiled back at her. And Lily realised what he was doing. He was helping because he thought the football ban was wrong, even though he didn't like football!

"The woods?" said the interviewer.

"The children have been playing in the woods," Mr Edwards told him. "They made a pitch. To play in secret."

"I have a great idea!" the TV interviewer said. "How about a game? In the woods? Teachers versus children. And if the teachers win, then football stays banned. And if the kids win, football is allowed!"

Some of the parents who had been listening in cheered. Mr Edwards looked at the ground as if he wanted it to open up and swallow him.

Then Mrs Baker put her hand on his arm.

He turned towards her.

She was nodding – telling him to agree.

Mr Edwards turned to the kids.

"Very well," he said, with a slight smile. "Teachers versus children. The winner takes it all."

Lily couldn't believe what had just taken place. Was this really going to happen?

The funny thing was, Mr Edwards had sounded pleased at the idea.

Chapter 16

Great Expectations

Six days later the woods were full. There were children and parents and the TV people were there too. They were going to film the challenge match of football that had captured the imagination of the whole city.

All week the children of Kingsfolly Junior had talked about nothing else. Could a team of Year 6s beat the teachers at football?

They were about to find out.

The children lined up in their strongest formation.

Zack

James　　　**Maddie**

Lily　　　**Batts**

Khal

Becky and Finn were subs.

On the teachers' team the strong players were Mr Luxton, the games teacher, in goal, Mrs Baker in defence and – up front – Mr Edwards himself and Mr Jones.

The TV interviewer had offered to referee the game. When she blew the whistle, a trio of pigeons took flight from the trees above the Secret Football Club's home ground.

The kids started well. They knew the pitch. And they knew each other. Lily, James and Khal had the ball for the first minute, passing it in triangles, making the teachers run around in circles.

Lily could hear people laughing because they thought it looked so easy.

Secret FC's first chance came after two minutes. Khal one-on-one with Mr Luxton in goal. But Khal – usually deadly one-on-one – scuffed the ball.

"What's up?" James asked. "That was a sitter!"

Lily walked over to them. She wanted everyone to stay positive.

"It's the cameras," Khal said. "They're making me nervous."

Lily and James looked over at the TV cameras. This game was going out on the local news that

night. All of a sudden Lily realised how strange this whole thing had become. The Secret Football Club was meant to be just that – a secret. Now it was going to be on TV.

The next time Khal got the ball near goal he passed it to Lily instead of shooting. Lily was so surprised that she missed the ball and let Mr Luxton pick it up and bowl it out to Mr Edwards.

Mr Edwards trapped the ball, turned and chipped it towards Zack's goal.

But Zack was looking at the TV camera too. Not the ball. And the first he knew about it was when it had bounced past him and Mr Edwards was jumping in the air, shouting in joy.

Goal!

The teachers were winning 1–0. And Lily realised that there was a good chance her team would lose this game.

Chapter 17

The Football Beast

At half-time it was still 1–0 to the teachers. And James was losing his cool.

"This is rubbish," he moaned. "We're losing to the teachers. We're losing our right to play football. And it's all going to be on TV tonight. I'm off."

Lily shook her head. "Don't give up now."

"Why not? This is embarrassing!"

Lily knew that if James left, they had no chance. They needed six players who really cared about

winning. She had to do something to make them gel as a team so they could win this game.

"James," Lily said. "I want you and Maddie to go up front. Me and Khal will drop back and defend. *You* can score the goals for us!"

James looked at her, saying nothing. Lily wondered if he understood or if he was about to disagree.

Then they heard Mr Edwards shouting for them to come back and play. And James surprised everybody.

"OK," he said. "I'll do it."

The new team looked like this.

Zack

Lily   **Khal**

Batts

James   **Maddie**

Suddenly the game was very different. Secret FC was on top. The teachers weren't getting a kick at all.

Two minutes into the second half Maddie passed to James, who ran towards the goal. He looked to have a chance of scoring.

But then Mr Edwards came lunging in to tackle him.

It looked like there was no way James could avoid the tackle.

But James somehow managed to skip over Mr Edwards, clipping the ball over his tackle too.

He'd done it. Done the impossible.

Now he was one-on-one against Mr Luxton.

He struck the ball. Hard.

When it flew through the air it was travelling so fast it seemed to whistle.

It was so fast that no one saw it until it came back off a large oak tree and hit the teachers' keeper on the back of the head. It was like the wood was on their side.

One all!

Lily leaped into the air. She felt like she was going mad. Maybe they *could* win this. Maybe they *would* be able to play football.

They only needed one more goal.

She could feel herself grinning. She looked at all her team-mates. They were all smiling too.

"COME ON!" she shouted. "This is it. We're going to win."

Chapter 18

Captain Fantastic

Mr Edwards kicked off after the equaliser.

He looked cross. Or was he excited?

Lily couldn't be sure.

She watched him tap the ball to Mrs Baker, who played it straight back to him. Then he started one of his runs, passing player after player. Only Batts's firm tackle stopped him giving the teachers the lead again.

The game was end-to-end.

Mr Edwards was making attack after attack. He was the only teacher who could really play. After he nearly scored again, Batts hoofed the ball up the pitch just to get it out of his way.

But James was at the end of Batts's long kick. He controlled the ball just right, side-stepped one teacher and slammed it past Mr Luxton.

2–1 to the kids. Lily couldn't believe it. She ran up to James and hugged him. Then everyone else did too.

As they broke up, James looked at Lily. "I'm sorry," he said.

"What for?"

"For giving away the secret."

They were sure that after that things would go well and they would go on to win and be allowed to play football again.

But it didn't.

A minute later the teachers equalised.

Mr Edwards again.

2–2.

"He's good," Maddie panted.

"I know," Lily replied.

There was a minute to go.

James had passed the ball back to Lily. And Lily played it to Maddie. But Maddie stumbled. Secret FC had lost the ball to Mr Jones.

Mr Jones wasted no time and played the ball to Mr Edwards, who ran at the goal, knowing there was barely any time left. He sprinted past Khal, then

past James, Batts and Lily, leaving Zack running out of his goal to reach the ball before the Head Teacher could shoot.

But it was not to be. Mr Edwards reached the ball and tapped it to the right of Zack. Zack fell to the ground, but he could only watch as Mr Edwards went past him on the left.

Then he heard him shout, "Goooooaaaaal!"

And it was. An easy tap-in. An open goal.

3–2.

It was over.

Chapter 19

Heroes

When the TV interviewer blew the final whistle,
Lily dropped to her knees and looked into the wood,
away from the TV cameras.

She loved this wood. And now she might never
be allowed into it again. And she would have to stop
playing football for ever.

Then she saw a hand reach down to her.

She looked up. It was Mr Edwards.

She took his hand. "Well played," she said, trying to be a good loser.

"Well played, you," said Mr Edwards.

Then he pointed to the TV camera. "They want you and me to do an interview. Will you come with me please?"

Lily didn't want to be interviewed by the TV. But because Mr Edwards had said 'please', she thought she should.

They walked together to the TV camera. It was only when they got there that Lily realised she was still holding Mr Edwards' hand.

"So, Lily," the interviewer said cheerfully. "You lost the game fair and square. Are you going to give up your protest?"

Lily nodded. And at the same time Mr Edwards spoke. "Yes, she is going to give up her protest."

Lily wondered what else he would say. Perhaps that she was going to be punished too?

"Because I am in awe of her."

The TV interviewer looked at Mr Edwards. "Really? What do you mean?"

Mr Edwards turned to address the parents and children and teachers, as well as the TV crew.

"*Who* are you in awe of?" the interviewer asked.

"Of Lily," Mr Edwards said. "And her friends." He cleared his throat. "How long did it take them to clear this wood to make a football pitch here? Weeks, I suspect. How creative have they been to find a way of doing something they love in secret? Very. I am in awe of them all."

Nobody spoke. It was like they were waiting for the punch line in a joke.

"From today, the school is going to invest in this football pitch," Mr Edwards said. "We are going to make it a little bit safer. And Lily and her friends are going to play on it as much as they like. As are the rest of the children at Kingsfolly Junior School."

Lily stared at her friends. They were all grinning. She looked at Mrs Baker, who smiled back at her too.

"I was wrong to ban football," Mr Edwards said. He gazed into the trees, as if he was looking for ideas among the leaves. "I was worried about danger and protecting the children. When I was young, a friend …" He stopped himself. "But that's another story. What I have learned this week is

that these children are special. They are talented and clever. They've had a real knock here – their favourite pastime taken away from them. And did they suffer? No. They thrived. They learned. They grew."

Mr Edwards turned to Lily and Khal and the rest of the Secret Football Club and spoke again.

"I'm sorry, children. I was wrong. If you'll let me, I'd like to be your team's number one fan."

Lily grinned.

And then she had an idea. A great idea. Mr Edwards was obviously very good at football ... He could help them!

"How about you become our coach?" she said.

Mr Edwards frowned. "I don't know much about coaching football. I'm not sure ..."

"You can play it, though, can't you?" said James. He put his arm round Lily. "We'd love it if you would be our coach."

After a moment's thought, with dozens of parents and teachers and pupils watching him, Mr Edwards nodded.

"Yes," he said. "Yes, please."

Turn over for more on *SECRET FC* ...

Football cards

All about the author

Fun 14th century facts

and

A top secret quiz!

All the facts about your favourite Secret FC players!

LILY ▶

Goals Scored	26
Height	132cm
Skill (1–10)	9
Speed (1–100)	73

ZACK ▶

Goals Scored	15
Height	136cm
Skill (1–10)	6
Speed (1–100)	81

JAMES ▶

Goals Scored	23
Height	152cm
Skill (1–10)	8
Speed (1–100)	86

BATTS ▶

Goals Scored	12
Height	140cm
Skill (1–10)	6
Speed (1–100)	76

MR EDWARDS ▶

Goals Scored	14
Height	170cm
Skill (1–10)	7
Speed (1–100)	64

MRS BAKER ▶

Goals Scored	9
Height	165cm
Skill (1–10)	5
Speed (1–100)	58

KHAL ▶

Goals Scored	21
Height	148cm
Skill (1–10)	7
Speed (1–100)	89

MADDIE ▶

Goals Scored	16
Height	138cm
Skill (1–10)	7
Speed (1–100)	68

All about the author

What gave you the idea for *Secret FC*?

I visit a lot of schools to talk about my books. Sometimes I find myself at schools where football is banned. Usually it's because the school doesn't have a lot of playground space and the teachers are worried about the little kids getting hurt by the big kids. It made me wonder what would happen if the children refused to accept a football ban.

Are the characters in *Secret FC* based on real people?

They are. Lily is based on my daughter. She features in some of my other books too. Mrs Baker is based on a teacher I know from Essex, and James is a boy from her school. I love putting real people in my books. It's a great way of making up a character.

Does your daughter like football, then?

Yes. She used to play football at her primary school, but now she likes rugby more! And she does fell running, like me.

Did she like *Secret FC*?

I think so – and I know that she likes being a character in the book. And she likes that there are other girls in it too. It's good not just to have boys in football books! Girls' football is the fastest-growing sport in the UK – that's one reason why Maddie and Lily are the main characters in *Secret FC*.

Do you agree that football should be banned?

No, I do not. A lot of schools I go to stagger play time to keep the younger and older children apart. Teachers have to look after the children's safety. But they know that girls and boys love to play football – or anything – at break, because it's fun and a good chance to practise their football skills!

Mr Edwards has a secret reason for banning football. Why did you include that in the book?

We learn that, when he was young, Mr Edwards had a friend who was badly injured playing football. It's no wonder he worries about children getting hurt. But he keeps his reason secret, so no one understands why he has banned the game. It's only when he tells people the painful truth that they can understand him.

Was that based on anything that happened to you?

Sort of. When I was 10, one of my friends rode fast through some long grass on his bike and hit a big rock. He was thrown off and broke some bones. I was there and it was horrible. The ambulance had to drive onto the field. But my friend was lucky. He got better, unlike Mr Edwards' friend.

Is there a history of football being banned?

Yes. I'd read about the real King Edward, who – so the story goes – banned mob football in 1314 because he wanted men to be practising their archery. I liked the idea of the king decreeing what sports people could and couldn't play. The idea of sports being banned sounds crazy – but it happens. Do you know of anywhere that sport is banned now? And why?

What is mob football?

Before football existed as we know it today, village teams used to play each other across great expanses of fields and streams. It was played on national holidays – and still is in some places. I think it'd be brilliant fun to play in a game of mob football like that. It sounds ace – although Mr Edwards would think it was very dangerous too!

Party like it's 1317!

You'd never be bored in the 14th century — try these fun pastimes!

- A wild, day-long game of mob football*
- Tune up your lute and sing a song
- A sedate game of chess
- Play "bob-apple" at Halloween
- A ride through the royal forest to hunt stags and wild boars

It was feast (for the rich) and famine (for the poor). Can you rustle up these snacks?

- Bread made from wheat gone mouldy
- Stone soup – a "pottage" with not much in it
- A huge meat pie made from 1 roe deer, 10 pigeons, 1 rabbit, 6 chickens and 26 hard-boiled eggs
- A vegetable broth called "skirrets and pasternacks"

Even though the King had banned it in 1314!

Life and death

It was important to have fun while you could because the 14th century was a dangerous time to live in! People liked to carry written charms to protect against death from fighting, fire, fever, storms and poison. Here is one such charm.

> May the King of the
>   elements protect me
>
> From the powder of venom
>
> From little sparks of fire
>
> From flint and from arrow
>
> From the sharp-blade knife
>
> And the keen edge
>   of the sword.

Do you think charms worked against these common causes of death?*

The Black Death

The bubonic plague was carried by fleas found on rats. Yuck! It killed up to half the population of Europe.

Childbirth

Extremely perilous for all women, rich and poor. Midwives with lots of experience looked after women in labour, but their equipment was very basic and many women who survived childbirth later died from infections.

Childhood

About a third of all children didn't reach their 7th birthday. They died of malnutrition, infection, accidents and diseases such as measles, smallpox and the flu.

* Unfortunately, no. UK life expectancy was about 24 years for men and 33 years for women.

QUIZ

Football is a very simple sport. But its rules are important! Take this quiz to find out how well you know them ...

1. What shape must a football pitch be?

(a) A square

(b) A rectangle

(c) A circle

2. What size is a standard football for professional matches?

(a) Size 5

(b) Size 0

(c) Size 10

How many subs are you allowed in a match?

(a) Three

(b) None

(c) As many as you want

Who is allowed to use their hands in a football match?

(a) Defenders and the goalie

(b) No one

(c) Only the goalie

When is a goal not a goal?

(a) When it's scored against your own goalie

(b) When the ball doesn't cross the line completely

(c) When the goalie is away from their goal

Answers

1(b) | 2(a) | 3(a) | 4(c) | 5(b)

Did you get all these right? If not, then go and play football in secret until you do!

If you love football, you'll love ...

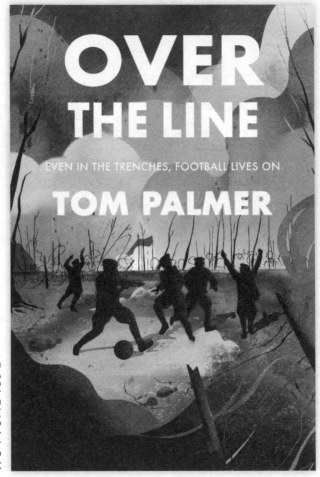

978-1-78112-956-2

For 90 minutes I forgot the shellfire, the rats, the Germans, the rain, the cold and the fear I felt when I was above the parapet, listening to the night.

Based on the true story of a sporting hero's experience in the trenches.

Tom Palmer visited all the significant places where the action of *Over the Line* happens. You can watch the videos on Reading War to find out about the trenches, see the locations in the novel and learn a song that soldiers sang to keep their spirits up.

Reading War is an online resource packed with information on the First World War.

www.readingwar.co.uk